# FORBIDDEN ISLAND

A Journey Beyond The Spotlight

I0665205

# FORBIDDEN ISLAND

A Journey Beyond The Spotlight

By Vida Xscape

From the **BOARDROOM** to the **XSCAPE LOUNGE;**

Where Rolexes and Stilettos co-exist!

# FORBIDDEN ISLAND

Copyright © 2012, 2019
Mahogany Vida Unlimited, LLC

Vida Xscape Books may be ordered through

Booksellers or by contacting:

Vida Xscape

2913 El Camino Real, #129

Tustin, CA  92782

https://vidascape.com

By Mahogany Vida Unlimited, LLC

Printed in the United States of America

Edited by Deborah McGill & Jon Mykal

Cover by Jon Mykal

# FORBIDDEN ISLAND

A Journey Beyond The Spotlight

## By Vida Xscape

This book is dedicated to all those who constantly juggle "busy" schedules and live "active" lifestyles.

Enjoy this book as you unwind and embrace a Journey full of "fun, laughter and romance," if only for a moment, "Beyond the Spotlight…"

# WELCOME

"Welcome," the sign read on the right hand side of the well-paved, marble stone road. Guests from every spectrum within the professional arena, from every corner of the world, entered through the gigantic, black, wrought iron gates. In huge, gold-plated letters the gate read, "Forbidden Island Resort."

As personal resort chauffeurs drove the Elite in groups of five around the spiral curved driveway, they were surrounded by the natural beauty of the island. From tall green trees and colorful, exotic plants to the two and four-legged creatures that ran amuck on the 4000 acre private, property; guests remained silent as they looked from one side to the other hoping not to miss a glimpse of the spectacular scenery.

As guests arrived at their final destination, they were both stunned and overwhelmed at the size, beauty and detailed architecture of the Forbidden Island Resort; a picturesque, postcard view reflecting an enormous castle, enclosing the wonders of nature, and a big body of water that bordered every inch of the perimeter.

Each and every guest was a highly established expert and mogul within their own profession; each hoping to get their Mahogany Vida In Check on this Forbidden Island getaway. They knew that plain commoners wouldn't understand what that meant – Getting Their Mahogany Vida In Check. But, to them, it meant "their identity." It meant, knowing who they were, where they came from, where they are going and not allowing anyone or anything to stop them or get in their way.

Getting their Mahogany Vida in check meant: that they knew their past and the challenges they've had to endure, although at times they may have to cry, pray, and have their pity-party in silence and/or in private; that they continue to have faith and belief in their dreams and goals even when no one else supports, understands, or lifts them up; and that they continue to have the perseverance, know-how and determination to excel and succeed in what they want for their lives personally, professionally and privately regardless of the barriers and challenges set forth before them; as nothing (including emotions) or no one (including a stranger) is going to get in their way.

# Searching For Self

The weather was blazing hot, yet a slight breeze filled the atmosphere as Yolie, a famous recording artist from Europe, laid poolside. She was secluded behind the large palm trees, red and yellow Stargazer flowers, ferns and other vibrant colored, tropical terrain plants. Basking in the sun's rays, in her mint green, low-rise bikini which so eloquently showed off her thick caramel curves, she was trying to lose herself on the "forbidden" exotic island -- away from work, away from paparazzi, away from adoring fans and away from all who knew and loved her. On this Island she knew no one would know her, and her identity would be concealed. She was told to leave her laptop, her briefcase and any traces of business behind, as for the next seven days she would both lose and find herself all at the same time.

As she drifted off into a peaceful slumber, in her private cabana, the mahogany ceiling fan slowly twirling above kept her cool, while the soothing sounds of water trickling down the red rock fountain, into the shallow pool below, kept her calm. There Yolie lay, as still as an ebony portrait just waiting to be admired. On the padded beige and burgundy colored lounge chair, an empty champagne glass set table top and the mellow sounds of Grover Washington Jr. softly played on the loud speaker overhead. Her oversized mint green hat perfectly flopped over her forehead, eliminating any sunlight from striking her unblemished, oval, brown face. While dozing off, she fell into the same dream she had so many times before — the perfect man, the perfect date and the perfect hideaway, yet the dream was somehow never complete. Once again, she was awakened, losing all memory of the details with only the feelings and emotions embedded so deep within her.

Feelings she not only yearned to experience, but emotions she could not fathom to verbally express to anyone in the outside world, for fear they would taunt her and not understand.

Drisco, a handsome Bohemian waiter quietly approached her. Carefully reaching out to touch her sultry skin in hopes of not startling her as she slumbered, he softly spoke to her. Disoriented from being awakened by his voice, Yolie began to open her beautiful eyes as he gently touched her shoulder with a simple glide across her skin.

In a strong accent, yet soft tone, Drisco said, "Excuse, me, but the gentleman over there would like to buy you a drink. What can I get for you?" Drisco gestured over to the private bar on the far right side of the pool.

With the sound of Drisco's voice, Yolie blinked, unconsciously squinting her eyes, trying to focus as she lifted her large brim, but couldn't with the sun beaming directly down on her. Still in a bit of a slumber, she lifted her hat once again; this time with the tips of her french tip nails so precisely manicured, but still had difficulty focusing. Raising her big black glasses with diamonds embedded in the frame, she gently rubbed her light brown eyes and glanced back at the bar, where a gentleman of grand stature and athletic build sat in his stark white linen lounge attire, sipping his half-full glass of scotch. With one foot propped up loosely on the stool's footrest, and the other secured firmly on the ground, he displayed patience as he waited for the precise moment when his eyes would meet hers.  As their eyes met, the gentleman raised his glass toward her with a slight nod of the head, smiling innocently leaving her in a hypnotic trance.

"Ma'am," Drisco tried to get Yolie's attention, but she didn't respond. "Excuse me, Ma'am. Are you all right?" Drisco tried again, this time breaking the spell

"Oh, yes," Yolie hesitantly responded as she briefly looked up at Drisco while glancing back at the gentleman at the bar, with a partially condensed, innocent smile. This was unlike Yolie. Yolie was known for being outgoing, boisterous and confident, but now displayed signs of being naïve, shy and childlike.

Before Yolie could answer, the man had already gotten up from the bar and approached her. He stood beside her blocking the blind spot she once had from the sun's rays, and eloquently introduced himself.

"I don't mean to bother you but you look very familiar to me. My name is Aaron." Aaron was from the States and was one of the top financial analysts to the stars and ran one of the most prestigious firms in the country. He was vacationing on the island to gain insight into whether he wanted to continue to pursue his practice or change occupations so he could live a "normal" life – away from the hustle and bustle of politics, entertainment, lengthy business deals and less than perfect partnerships. Entranced by her beauty, he gazed hypnotically into her eyes and she into his, this time both looking as though they could read each other's most intimate thoughts. Forgetting that he had already asked, Aaron asked again if he could join her. Yolie tried to respond but couldn't. She opened her mouth but nothing came out. All she could do was continue to gaze into his dark brown eyes. She began transferring her contact between his dreamy eyes and his well- sculptured, thick lips.  Oh the things he could do with those lips she thought to herself. Realizing her thoughts may be open for public display as she internally visualized his lips touching hers, kissing and engulfing the different parts of every inch of her body parts, she blushed, tilting her head to the side while biting the corner edge of her bottom lip.

Aaron noticed Yolie's facial expressions and smiled at the mere thought of what she could possibly be thinking or he could definitely be doing. As Yolie continued to gaze in Aaron's eyes she suddenly blushed as she realized that he was the man embedded in her dreams. The man she unleashed herself too, the man who knew her innermost thoughts, aspirations and journey. She questioned herself whether she was still in a dream or was this reality.

Finally, gathering her thoughts, she hesitantly responded, "hello yourself. Yes, please join me." She paused, praying he would say something; worried she was staring; or that he could see right through her. Nothing was said and nothing needed to be. Anything that could possibly be stated in that instant was already transparent through their magnetism; and it was at that moment that time stood still.

Porsche, Yolie's best friend since childhood, was lingering inside the resort lobby at the bar. She was busy scoping out the territory with her short, orange wraparound skirt and matching bikini top. She was looking for a man, any man to get lost with, away from any and all obligations, including that of her title as Yolie's Personal Assistant. For the next seven days she carried no title but best friend, and prior to their departure that agreement was set in stone after several glasses of Long Island Ice Teas and a few hatch backs of Strawberry Jell-O Shooters.

While sitting at the bar with legs crossed, cleavage stuck out and one side of her hip sauntered just a tad to the left, Porsche, with her eagle eye watched as men checked in solo, as well as with companions, trying to get the lay of the land. This would be "their" opportunity; "their" privilege to meet her versus the other way around. Each time she saw someone with potential, she would swivel her chair just enough for him to get the backside view of her thick thighs, big hips and elongated curvature.

During this process, she'd add a little zest, a little pop, as she sensually stirred her Mai Tai with the tip of her straw, not only adding flavor to the drink but a nonverbal, open invitation to join her, of which she was confident no man in their right mind could resist.

Those with swagger and heighted interest would generously receive Porsche's rendition of how to partake of a sliced pineapple in such a way nothing was left to the imagination. Others would merely get the PG13 version, just for enticement purposes, giving her the power to have control; at least in her eyes. She couldn't fathom the concept they just might not be interested in her. No, that would never happen.

As she continued to sit at the bar admiring all the eye-candy, a tall yet stocky gentleman approached from behind. He had been observing Porsche in her bright orange from the time she entered the bar and watched her talent go to work from the chair swivels to the pineapple consumption.

"Is this seat taken," he said, startling Porsche and throwing her off her game.

Swiveling to the left, to get a visual of the person behind the voice, she uncomfortably stuttered, "Uh, no, feel free." Pulling herself together, she motioned with her hands her approval of him to grace her with his presence and join her, but the confidence or lack thereof fell short very quickly. Smiling, almost embarrassed that she was caught by surprise and undecided as to how well she pulled off her unorthodox attempt to be passive and naïve, Porsche tried to maintain her decorum. She shook her long, dark, brown hair, combing it backward ever so slightly with her fingertips and smiled once again, this time sensual in nature.

"Thank you," he responded with a devilish smile as he slowly scanned her dark thick curvatures with eyes that were undeniably engulfed with unspoken words. Slowly looking away, he tried to get the bartender's attention. With confidence, he lifted his hand with his right index finger pointing upward and placed his order. "Uh, rum and coke please," he said in his raspy baritone voice.

With eyes refocused on Porsche, he caught her biting

the index finger on her right hand as she leaned back sizing him up, while strategically calculating his backside from the top of his large 22 inch neck, to his strong bulging biceps, right down to his perfectly shaped apple bottom. His cut, that was planted so nicely on the bar stool beside her, covered all remnants of the black charcoal leather seating which was definitely a dish for partaking. "Ummm, how I would love to see what is under that," she mumbled to herself with a small chuckle.

Timeless hours had gone by and Yolie realized she was late meeting Porsche for lunch. Apologizing to Aaron for having to cut their encounter short, she hesitantly excused herself from his presence, but not without telling him how much she enjoyed meeting him as well as his company. Aaron, not wanting the moment to end, swiftly yet tenderly grabbed her hand as she got up to gather her belongings that laid at the edge of the pool.

"I know you need to go, but would you do me the honor of having dinner with me tonight?" Aaron appeared confident and self-assured, even though inside he was praying on bended knee that she would accept his invitation.

"Do me the honor," she questionably repeated to

herself, "who says that…?" No matter how corny it appeared to have sounded, she thought it was sweet and she was excited. She slowly nodded, with a half smile, gathered the remainder of her things, and headed toward the hotel's glass lobby doors.

Slowly walking back towards the lounge, Yolie's hips swayed just a little bit more that afternoon. With each step, her hips swerved to the beat of a different kind of drum portraying their own rhythmic pattern of Ba Boom Boom – Ba Boom Boom – Ba Boom Boom; an integral beat only she knew how to do.

Consciously unaware, she walked right past Porsche sitting at the bar, beyond the bright tropical flowerpots, to the large elevator doors. Slowly sliding her room key card down the passage to enable the elevator to work, she pushed the up button, in a daze, as she stared at the image of herself in the mirrored elevator walls but the only reflection she saw back was the figment of the man in her dream; was it possibly Aaron?

Entering her Executive Suite, she stumbled over her belongings as she tried to gather her bearings between her bottle of water, green lounge bag, BWEE Magazine and room key card. Gathering them up once again, she swiftly moved over to the large chaise lounge, adjacent to the bed, and dropped everything before they slipped away from her. She then sauntered over to the oversized king bed draped in burgundy and gold and fell backwards with her arms up entrusting the soft but firm mattress and satin sheets to catch and embrace her.

Without a moment to spare Porsche knocked on the door, questioning Yolie about the dude by the pool and why she walked right past her, at the bar, as if she didn't see her. But, before Yolie could get a word in edge wise, Porsche interrupted depicting her overdramatized version of the men who tried to pick her up but had no game.

"Girl, let me tell you," Porsche said. "I was just sitting there minding my own business and guys just kept approaching me, licking their lips and stuff, talking about I'll drink your bath water. Girl, can you believe that?"

Sitting on the edge of the bed, Porsche crossed her legs, like a debutante, as she leaned to the side swinging her hair only to expose her bare neck. To add a touch of sensuality to her story she slid the palm of her hand down her smoothly shaven legs and without intent lost it as she unintentionally sucked her lips together making a loud smacking sound.

"Well, you know how I do it," Porsche arrogantly said lifting her right hand and swinging it downward as if she were swatting a pesky fly while taking a saucy step forward. Yolie didn't say a word.

"Some of these guys are fine as hell but they just got no game." Yolie was not amused and not in the mood to hear or partake of one of Porsche's antics, thereby allowing her mind to drift off and lay elsewhere.

With every word Porsche spoke, she had an over exaggerated facial expression to match. Sticking out her derrière and rubbing her hand over her thick curves, she continued, "Shoot, they can't handle all of thissss." All Yolie could do was shake her head and smile as she knew Porsche was a hot mess since they were kids and there was no controlling her even then, so why even try now.

Feeling a bit exhausted from the sun, the pool and the unexpected encounter with Aaron, Yolie decided to take a nap but not without controversy from Porsche regarding breaking their lunch plans. After a ten minute cat nap, Porsche and Yolie decided to forgo lunch since the time had surpassed and dinner was right around the corner.

Porsche adjourned into the neighboring Suite to get ready for the evening's festivities of drinks, dinner and dancing. Yolie sat perplexed on the plush, crème couch remaining silent, not wanting to uncover the details of her encounter with Aaron, at least not yet.  Not until she could make some sense of it all, as she knew Porsche would not only have more than a few choice words for her, but would also embarrass her with her boisterous personality, and that was definitely what she wanted to prevent.

As Yolie continued to lounge on her couch, she thought about her conversation with Aaron and wondered why she felt sooo… different; an emotion she couldn't quite put her finger on. She began to question her emotions and question the mere reality of whether this was indeed a figment of her imagination. Self-doubt set in along with fear, not wanting to get hurt yet at the same time, not wanting to miss this potential opportunity. Of what, she didn't know, only felt.

She wandered into the bathroom to splash some cool water on her face hoping that would wake her up, give her a sign, or wash away any feelings of doubt and insecurity. As she gazed into the mirror she asked herself, "What am I doing? Am I crazy? Uggg!" Posing questions came at her left and right, but all she could do was look at her reflection in the wide-length mirror and smile at the simple feeling of...

# Unspoken

Downstairs just past the elevator corridors and beyond the concierge, the music had already started. Guests were congregating at the bar, mingling in the lobby and lining up for dinner for the evening's festivities. The waiters were in place and the food was in its respective bins ready to be served. Men were decked in cool, linen multi-colored suits while women were dressed to impress, leaving very little to the imagination, from backless dresses that stopped just beyond their ba dunk ka dunks, to exposed cleavage-bound minis that barely covered all of their morning glory.

Porsche was still upstairs putting the final touches on her next-to- nothing cocktail dress. She wore her hair pulled back in a high, Shirley Temple Ponytail that showed off her oversized diamond hoop earrings and accessorized the rest of her ensemble with ringlets of bangles and a long gold necklace that draped from her neck down to her diamond tear drop belly ring only to loosely circle her thick shapely hips and reconnect in the center of her ring. Taking one last glance in the mirror, she moved from side to side as she sized up her body from head to toe. She used her hands as she slowly and gently smoothed out wrinkles, unapparent to the naked eye, with elongated strokes across her breasts, down her sides, and over her lower extremities. "Nice," she said as she grabbed her purse and strolled out the door.

Knocking on Yolie's door, Porsche was excited, anxious and ready to get her groove on. She stood and waited, but Yolie didn't answer. Knocking again, this time more forcefully, she decided to add some volume hoping to gain some attention.

"Yolie," open up, let's go." Still, no answer. Yolie was completely unaware to the ruckus Porsche was creating outside her Suite. With earphones on, she was hidden away in her private sanctuary, surrounded by lavender scented bubbles and smooth R&B. Only time would tell if her cat nap mixed with a warm bath and mellow music would calm her nerves.

An hour or so had gone by before Yolie removed her pruned brown skin from the warm bath water. Getting out, carefully stepping onto the circular, plush bath mat laid directly in front of her sunken Jacuzzi bathtub, she was oblivious to the time as she knew that was all she had a lot of... time.

Reaching for the baby oil with aloe vera, she poured just enough on her hands to rub and smear it all over her wet sultry skin leaving no spot untouched, paying special attention to her breasts, inner thighs, backside and legs. Grabbing the king sized towel that hung on the side panel of the marble wall, she slowly dried herself off, while checking to make sure all was smooth in all the right places. Once dry, she kept her remedy of moisturizing her entire body from head to toe with her custom-made lotion.

She continued prepping herself spraying citrus Body Splash on her inner wrist, neck, breasts, and inner thighs and then ruffled through her closet for something tantalizing, sassy yet classy to wear. Something that would make a statement, was sexy, and would leave her confident all at the same time.

Downstairs encompassed an array of activities, with guests dining, dancing, and mingling and amongst them was Porsche. She waited for no man, including Yolie, and had already scoped out the layout of the land.  Porsche was at the bar sipping any and all sweet alcoholic beverages offered or available for consumption. She was the life of the party with an entourage of men groveling at her feet just hoping to get a dance, or even just moment of meaningless conversation with her.

Laughing and talking in her flirtatious ways, she caught the eye of Yolie who had just stepped out of the elevator. "Wow! Now **that's** my girl," she said. With the biggest of grins, she redirected the focus from herself onto Yolie as she signaled her with a wave of her arms to come over and join her and her menzzz.

"Uh, Kem, right?" Porsche said inquisitively. "Can you be a dear and scoot over just a tad?" Kem looked confused and couldn't understand why Porsche just brushed him to the side when he thought he was making some headway, especially after just buying her yet another drink. The other men looked just as baffled as Kem did but that feeling was short lived. Once they realized the focus of Porsche's attention, clarity swiftly set in with each and every one of them almost instantaneously.

"Hey girl, it's about time you came down," Porsche said loudly as she grabbed Yolie's hand prompting her to sit in the seat beside her. No faster did those words come out of her mouth when the volume of the bar became a little softer that evening and the vibe of the room became a little more focused.

The spotlight was bright and from the crescent-shaped bar to the octagon-shaped restaurant; all eyes were centered on Yolie as though she were center stage about to perform. There she stood vibrant as ever in her exotically sexy, red cocktail dress showing off each and every one of her natural curves that went for days and long smooth bare legs so vividly revealed in her 3 inch red stilettos. Her hair nicely layered and curled lay just above her bra line while her perfectly applied make-up was evenly shaded in natural earth tones.

Mouths were open, ears were heightened, and testosterone levels were elevated as everyone tried to make room to get just a glimpse of this womanly sensation. Women bared witness, not in hatred, but in awe of how one woman could solely reap the attention of every living being in the room, young and old, without even trying.

Yolie graciously smiled at all the attention but was not impressed, not like Porsche. Attention was something she always had and hoped she had left behind, in Canada. And although no one knew her from the entertainment realm, having people gawk at her feet was not within her comfort zone, especially when she wasn't in character and not on stage. No, she had one thing on her mind and one thing only. She wanted more time with Aaron.

"Can I get you something?" a familiar voice asked breaking Yolie's feeling of uneasiness and pressure to feel like she had to do something spectacular, sing a song or be unnaturally caddy. Turning her head, Yolie recognized her waiter by the pool. It was Drisco, but this time he was behind the bar.

"Hi." Yolie smiled, as she sighed a breath of calming relief from hearing that familiar accent and seeing that familiar face. "So, you're a bartender too huh?" Yolie nodded, appearing impressed and glad to have someone to talk to, someone familiar outside of the island meat market that surrounded her, the market that Porsche so genuinely enjoyed.

"Yes, I do a little bit of everything around here," Drisco said modestly with a wide-eyed grin. "So, what can I get for you, while you wait? My treat. How about some Stella Island Rose?"

"That would be great, thank you." Smiling, Yolie watched Drisco open a brand new bottle of wine, just for her, and pour just a touch into a wine glass for her to take the edge off.

"For mad' am Yolie – the Island Goddess." Drisco sarcastically said, smiling as he handed Yolie the glass for her approval. "Oh stop it," Yolie said with a chuckle seemingly a tad bit embarrassed, yet honored to be termed a Goddess, even if he was kidding. Taking a sip, Yolie nodded in approval, as Drisco continued pouring.

"Hey bartender, you wanna hook a sister up," Porsche said interrupting the moment in a sassy tone. Yolie couldn't believe Porsche just said that. Well, yes she could, but hoped she wouldn't have. Shaking her head as Drisco looked on, all Yolie could do was shrug her shoulders while Drisco grinned.

"Sure, no problem. Any friend of Yolie's is a friend of mine. Here you go. It's on the house." Drisco smiled, easing Yolie's embarrassment as if to say, "no worries, my friend. It's my pleasure."

Grabbing the glass of wine, Yolie said, "I'll drink to that," as she turned to the five gentlemen surrounding her. She raised her glass slightly in front of her and touched it up to the sky making sure she heard a clinking sound to each and everyone's glass before taking a sip of her own.

"Interesting friends you have Island Goddess," Drisco said with a smirk as he looked onward at Porsche and her posse break bread.

"Yeah, well, she has been my best friend since childhood so hey, what can I say. Gotta love her. Never a dull moment."

As they both laughed at Yolie's statement, the bar was filling up and the conversation was once again at maximum volume, that was until the song "Freak Me" came on, by Silk, and then that took the vibe to a whole other level. Porsche started singing "Freak me baby, ah yeah," and while you would think she went solo, she was indeed the leader of the pack. Other couples, groups and individuals chimed in and joined her singing the song in its entirety, bumping and grinding by the bar, swaying from side to side in the restaurant, while others tried to remember the dance it aligned itself with from yester year on the moderately sized, wooden dance floor.

As the song came to close, another familiar voice was heard from the shadows. "Yolie, there you are. I've been looking for you. Are you ready?" Aaron said, as he appeared from the other side of the bar extending his hand to hers.

Smiling, Yolie nodded and then looked back at Drisco to thank him, telling him she would talk to him later. Drisco nodded and watched her as she was led off to the restaurant.

Aaron was looking quite dapper in his beige with splotches of red accents complimenting Yolie's attire. But before she could leave the bar, Porsche made it a point to get her two cents in by mouthing "damn girl, it's like that?" All Yolie could do was smile with a simple eye gesture only she and Porsche understood, resembling the statement of, "uh, hell yes," as she gave Porsche a quick wink of the eye as if to say, don't wait up. And without further notice, Yolie was off following Aaron close behind toward their table for two.

During dinner, little verbal communication was heard. Beyond the little small talk, there was little to be said. Yolie found herself searching for things to say and trying to carry most of the conversation while watching people on the dance floor get their groove on. The unspoken words were more magnetic than those that were spoken as the physical attraction between them poured from every pore of their beings.

Noticing Yolie's focus on the dance floor, watching

guests and swaying to the music, he asked, "Do you want to dance?" Aaron's words appeared to be spoken at a snail's pace as if he were accentuating each syllable ensuring she could hear and understand what was being asked of her. The simple question appeared, in Yolie's eyes, more complex and although no words were exchanged, the mutual feeling was understood.

"I'd love to," Yolie said with a captivating grin, desiring to see what was next. Aaron assisted Yolie from the table and onto the dance floor. The energy between them was magnetic as though they were the only people dancing. Still words were left unsaid physically, but not mentally. Whether it was fast or slow, the music spoke for them and nothing else seemed to matter.

Porsche on the other hand was rump-shaking and earth-quaking all over the dance floor, regardless of the rhythm and beat. And, with each new partner, she had a new introduction and a new body move to show him. Porsche was having the time of her life, not being committed to any one individual; not worried about anyone seeing or knowing who she was; not living up to anyone's (especially Yolie's) professional standards; and shaking what her mother gave her.

Hours had gone by and it was getting late. Yolie had an early morning spa treatment and Aaron was quite tired and jet-lagged. Although the feeling of taking it to the next level was on the top of their minds, they decided to turn in and continue with their journey another day.

As Aaron escorted Yolie up to her suite, hand in hand, she could feel the intense emotions running through the palms of their hands. She wanted him, desired him but at the same time wanted to wait. Why? She didn't know.

Arriving at the entrance to her suite, he leaned in for a simple kiss but not before he kissed her hand thanking her for a wonderful evening. Smiling, Yolie felt tingly and special, yet surprised that he didn't ask to come in, nor request the date to last a little while longer.

Yolie adjourned into her room, threw off her stilettos and slowly walked out onto the balcony. The temperature was warm, registering approximately 80 degrees, but with the island breeze, it was comfortable and soothing, a nice day for an evening stroll. And even as she stood over her balcony taking in the evening's fresh air, she reminisced about the day's occurrences as she watched the colors of the pool change from pink to blue to green and white. Yolie looked to the left and watched a young couple holding each other tightly, embraced in each other's arms and then to the right, where the calming sounds of the waterfall created a spellbinding sculpture as another couple laid idle, holding hands, entranced in their own moment in time. It was serene, romantic and illuminating and all Yolie could do was smile and think to herself, this was her time.

# Forbidden Treatment

Its 7:00 in the morning and the alarm on the black Boeing Clock, sitting on the edge of the night stand, began to sound. Yolie, tired and still half asleep rolled over to turn it off but not without her right breast half unveiling itself, outside of her crème colored camisole, wondering if there was anyone within arm's reach who would be available to assist and comfort it, while bidding it a good morning but there was no one there -- just Yolie.

Extending her hand just a little more to turn on some Brian McKnight to start her day, she realized she only had two hours before her spa treatment.  Picking up the phone, she dialed Porsche's extension, but it went straight to voicemail. Laying in bed, just a little while longer, she began thinking about Aaron; when and if she would see him again.

Stumbling out of bed, still trying to wake up, Yolie completed her daily routine to prepare herself for the day's activities. Walking out of the door dressed in a black and white bikini and matching wrap, Yolie knocked on Porsche's door to see if she was going to join her. Waiting outside she could hear giggles and whispers coming from inside the room, however faint.

Opening the door, Porsche was dressed in an oversized chocolate bath towel with her hair looking like she had just stepped off of a rollercoaster.

"Uh, hey girl, what's up?" Porsche said trying to block any view inside the doorway.

"I was going to ask you if we were still on for breakfast but I see you've already haaaad your breakfast," Yolie said sarcastically as she smirked while peeking inside to see a dark, chocolate gentleman laying on the bed semi- exposing himself. "I'll catch you later," Yolie said as she shook her head at Porsche and walked off toward the elevator doors.

"Bye, yeah, uh, let's do lunch or something," Porsche, somewhat embarrassed, yelled back and, with each word, softer than the next. Looking down the mustard-colored corridor, Porsche took one last glance before re- entering her room to continue with her organic man-made breakfast.

Downstairs Yolie was quite content dining by herself on the outdoor patio. She had all she needed: a juicy book, some fresh strawberries, her freshly brewed island coffee, a ham, spinach and mushroom omelet, a slice of whole wheat toast, and a tall glass of orange juice. Every now and then she would glance up from her reading material to take a quick poll of her surroundings. She watched guests get served by handsome island natives, dressed in Bermuda shorts and short-sleeved, colorful shirts and observed the island's wildlife scanter across the grass as she took in the beautiful scenery. Taking in a deep long breath, she slowly closed her eyes, rested her head back on her chair, and enjoyed the tranquility as she partook of all the fresh island air.

Finishing her meal she was off to the spa but finding it was no easy task. The hotel's day spa was closed off in a little hideaway beyond the main lobby and looked as if it were completely separate from the island's private resort. Walking through exotic plants, birds of paradise, tall bamboo trees, palm trees and vines that lingered overhead, Yolie was captivated by the mysteriousness and beauty of it all.

She walked along running creeks and heard birds and crickets singing and communicating in the distance, but there was no one to ask for assistance; no one to show her the way; only the path before her would be what guided her in the right direction.

"You must be Yolie," a short, young, Bohemian woman said upon her entry into the frosted glass doors. "My name is Wodika and I will be assisting you this morning and preparing you for your treatment."

"Uh, yes, hi," Yolie said spellbound as she wondered how this woman, Wodika, knew her name. Wasn't anyone else registered, she thought to herself. Yolie smiled at the stocky woman as she sat down on the plush, burnt orange and burgundy reception chair and filled out the forms that were given to her.  Completing the last series of questions, she handed Wodika back the clipboard and said, "I like your accent." Smiling, Wodika nodded as if to say "thank you" and exchanged the clipboard for a tall glass of water filled with lemon and cucumbers.

"Have you had a massage here before," Wodika asked as she took the half drunken glass from Yolie's hands and handed her a short, white robe and a white, satin blindfold in which the word "forbidden" was stitched on the center backside in black.

"No, it's my first time." Yolie began getting nervous;

a robe; a blindfold.  What in the world did she just get herself into she wondered.

Sensing Yolie's nervousness, Wodika smiled again and began with Yolie's instructions.

"On this island, we help take you away from yourself and your life, if only for a moment while you are here. It is our mission to help you relax, find yourself and make sure you have a good time. Today, you will be given a one hour and thirty minute full body massage by Jace, one of our top specialists on the island. The key to enjoying it is unadulterated, nonverbal, full body communication. We know your physical, sexual and emotional interests, likes and dislikes, and comfort areas, based on the forms you completed, so we know, for example, the intensity level you would be comfortable with, your preferences, desires, and scents you favor. You will enjoy your massage and the experience, if you allow your mind and body to be free and clear of everything and anything. If you do this, our specialist will be able to read your body language, without talking, and adjust to your taste accordingly..."

Yolie began to relax as she continued to listen to Wodika's instructions and friendly demeanor. Although she was definitely stepping out of her comfort zone, Yolie made a conscious decision right then and there to just let everything go and enjoy the experience. After Wodika continued with the instructions, Yolie was escorted to a private cabana where she was to disrobe, put on her blindfold, lay on the white linen table face down, and wait.

Entering into the private cabana, Yolie was taken by its beauty. It wasn't just an ordinary room like in most spas in the States, Canada or Europe. No, this was different. This was an outdoor cabana that was hidden from view, not by four cemented walls but by the wonders of nature, plants and greenery in their natural habitat. Wildlife sounds continued to be heard in the distance, the same sounds she heard as she walked the forbidden path leading her to this establishment. Scented candles electrified the feeling of the room and smooth-sounding island music played softly overhead. The music appeared like a mixture of what Yolie would call a combination of jazz, calypso, and classical, baby-making music. The ambiance was perfect and Yolie couldn't wait to see what was going to happen next.

Entranced in the moment, Yolie decided to do a quick stubble check to make sure she was 100% in the moment before Jace, her private masseuse walked in. Legs, check; underarms, check; lower extremities, check, check and double check. She climbed onto the table, secured her weight and positioned herself accordingly, covered her eyes as instructed, moved her hair to one side exposing her bare shoulders and waited.

Minutes had gone, which seemed like hours and Yolie was phasing into a deep slumber. Her back was exposed from the waist up and she could feel a warm sensation hovering over her unclothed body. Without sound and without warning she felt a man's big strong hands gently rub the back of her shoulders and could smell and feel the warmth of the aromatherapy oils against her uncovered skin. He moved his hands to the top of her neckline while gently stirring away any stray hair that was within his path. As Jace continued, she could feel his hands communicating to her while moving down to her mid and lower back focusing a bit more time around her well-shaped bottom and forty- six inch hip-line.

Special attention was given as he slowly uncovered one leg and gently spread her legs open with the wedge of his hand, but only enough to tuck the 400-count linen sheet securely underneath the other. It was at that moment when she took in a deep breath and exhaled. She wanted so badly to turn over and take a quick peek to see what Jace looked like; the visitor who was so close to her pulsating nectar but promised herself that no matter what happened, she would abide by the house rules and not ruin the experience.

Slowly lifting her right leg, Jace began to massage her calves and feet gently yet firmly. As he moved upward to her inner thighs, Yolie's nectar began to moisten as she closed her eyes tighter, inside the blindfold, to embrace all the emotions, feelings and sensations Jace and his hands had to offer. She softly moaned in delight as she grabbed the edges of the sheet while he compressed the palms of his hands over her bottom once again but this time he had ventured downward into unfamiliar territory; just below the opening within her crevice, and there he lingered but didn't go in. Yolie could feel a sense of warm heavens surrounding her as her vaginal lips opened just a little more, yearning for the welcomed attention as Jace worked his magic. He continued with the other leg enticing her to beg for more as surges of electricity scoured within and throughout her body.

Filtering whatever deposits that may have leaked onto

the top of her inner thigh; Jace swiftly removed any fluid bearing not to lay witness as he re- covered her back with the sheet while assisting her to turn over utilizing any and all non-verbal communication.

Before he began phase two, he quietly checked Yolie's blindfold for any signs of visuals, re-centered her on the stretched out table, and lifted her hair ever so gently from behind her neck so that it lay loosely on the backside of the table toward the floor. As he did this, Yolie could feel his bare skin lean upon hers as he bent forward to prep her. At that moment, she exhaled once more, as her mind wandered into a whole different dimension.

Once secured, Jace slowly lowered the sheet again but this time it was resting loosely over Yolie's breasts. And as he lowered it, he simultaneously replaced it by brushing a soft piece of satin cloth, the size of a hand towel, across her, breasts just enough to cover the outer lining of her size C cup.

Yolie, aroused by the feeling of being semi-exposed, took in another deep breath as she arched her back hoping not to display any signs of weakness and excitement yet unconsciously hoping to expose a little more skin outside the rectangular sized cloth. She wanted to entice and encourage Jace to expand on his internal skill set, should he choose to do so. It was at that moment, when she recovered her back to its natural flat state, that she licked her lips to display her sense of enjoyment and yearning for more.

Smiling at Yolie's response, Jace continued to gradually lower the sheet to her waistline. He rubbed his hands together and went to work starting with upper body. This was the perfect opportunity, Yolie thought; to see this man who's attained her undivided attention; whose ongoing non-contact, sexual stimulation has taken her to an extreme she's never felt. Yolie so wanted him to touch her, caress her and stimulate her in, in any and every way a human could imagine beyond the corridors of this room; beyond the one hour and thirty minute timeframe; and beyond any stipulation incurred by standard staff rules and regulations.

Next was the emphasis on the temporal lobes, her right and left temple, and the outer lining of her flawless brown face. Yolie relaxed, breathed out as he caressed the outer and under layer of her full breasts lingering down her ribcage to her stomach where he continued to make contact with every inch of her skin massaging, caressing and touching while being attentive and allowing her to be poetically submissive.

His flavor was so hot and transparent that Yolie could feel Jace's own temperature rising against her naked skin as he continued to unconsciously and accidently rub up against her as he tendered to every section of her body. He so wanted to please her internally as well as externally but kept his position, as it wasn't the time to move beyond the external kingdom.

It was now time to concentrate on her lower extremities, and although he was wound up yearning to take things to a completely different and deeper level, he barred down and remained focused. As he slowly removed the sheet from Yolie's waistline, he concurrently added a replacement similar to that of the cloth on her breasts. He looked intense as he massaged her thick thighs and as he lifted each to stretch his big hands underneath, to grab a secure hold before the next process were to begin, he accidently touched the edge of her nectar's wall. Yolie without hesitation arched her back once again in excitement and then seductively opened her legs, nonverbally hoping he'd accept the invitation to enter.

Jace was fighting back the temptation, and it was all he could do not to accept Yolie's open invitation but loved how she was able to communicate so effectively her wants and desires. He knew there were no rules in her forbidden treatment, but wanted so desperately to give her something more than just sexual interaction; he wanted to give her the sense of what she deserved based on the information sheet she filled out, but oh how difficult it was.

Knowing she wasn't allowed to speak or remove the forbidden blindfold, her body took over the conversation of her mouth and her eyes. With the sheer touch of Jace's hands glossing across her nectar's wall once again "accidently," her body instantly reacted by a smooth shift in her positioning, unveiling a portion of her bare nectar which yearned for his attention. Seeing her cleanly shaven nectar, Jace was mesmerized and wanted so bad to partake of the forbidden fruit. All of his bodily functions said yes, but his heart and mind said, no… just wait.

Instead of reacting to his own needs, all he wanted to do was satisfy her and finish what he started.  As he took a deep breath, he couldn't take his eyes off of her body, especially that which was now exposed.  He was so glad that she was blindfolded and could not see the expressions on his face nor the rise in his shorts.  All Yolie could do was feel the power of his energy upon hers as he continued with her massage.

Continuing to watch her pulsating nectar, he concentrated his energy on the area that mattered most to her at that moment.  With more oil on his hands he massaged the entire area, including her outer walls and interior lining paying close attention to her bare lips that opened automatically with the touch of his hands, welcoming forbidden visitors to take suit. Jace increased his surveillance area to the outer perimeters of Yolie's thighs only to touch bases in the entry way from time to time, as if he was lurking and waiting for something to take hold, but never in still motion.

He continued to venture across the rest of her body, always returning to the hub, her nectar, for feedback and approval. Once completed, Jace placed a white, plush, oversized, warm towel over her body following the removal of the two bite size cloths meant to cover her earthly possessions. He smoothed his well-skilled hands for the last time over her upper, mid, and lower extremities, placed them at peace upon her stomach for a few seconds ending her session, and then shook his head looking at her, desiring her and wanting her, as he quietly walked out of the door.

Yolie was relaxed, excited, curious and horny all at the same time. She so wanted to experience some unadulterated sexual stimulation during and after her massage while at the same time was thankful for the respect that was given to her by Jace. After she laid there for a few moments, Yolie slowly sat up and looked around almost in a dazed state, as if the wind was knocked out of her.

"Damn, if this is how I'm feeling now, I can only imagine how it would be if he really did make love to me," she said to herself.

Beside her, on the counter, was a tall glass of cold water with lemon and cucumber; the best water at that moment she'd ever tasted. The note read, "It was wonderful making your acquaintance and I hope you enjoyed yourself. See you soon!  Jace."

All Yolie could do was smile as she read the note and drank her water. "Are you kidding," Yolie thought to herself as she got dressed and wandered back into the lobby.

"Ms Yolie, how was your massage," Wodika asked grinning from ear to ear as though she could either read her thoughts or was privy to a hidden video camera that recorded particular evidence that would accuse her of a crime.

Blushing, Yolie answered, "It was wonderful thank you." Pausing for a brief moment, Yolie looked at Wodika like she was caught with her fingers in the cookie jar. "Is Jace available, I'd really like to thank him?"

Smiling bigger, Wodika shook her head "no" and stated that she would give him the message. Disappointed, that she never got a chance to physically meet Jace eye to eye, Yolie left the Spa, but not without the fond memories of her forbidden treatment.

# The Basement

As Yolie underwent forbidden treatment at the Spa, Porsche was busy doing due diligence as a DIVA. She was basking in the glory of being spoiled and spoon-fed from the previous night before to the early morning hours. Following her organic man-made breakfast, she was then treated to a second round, but this time publicly in the downstairs restaurant. Finishing her fruit- filled waffles, coffee, and sausage rounds with biscuits and gravy, she excused herself from her overnight guest, but not before kissing him on the cheek with pending plans to reunite at a later time.

Leaving, Porsche found her way to the far side of the lobby where a group of guests gathered for a private wine-tasting event. Dressed in a colorful, strapless mini, Porsche mingled amongst the guests and took what she would describe as her rightful place among several men who looked and personified the sheer image of wealth. As she struck up a conversation with each one individually, she captivated their attention with the swing of her hair, her sensual stance, her riveting laugh, the batting of her eyes, and her innocent, yet seductive grin. The small talk amongst the crowd and authentic island music playing overhead kept the guests occupied before they were permitted to go in.

The hostess, dressed in black and beige, in a stunningly slim business- casual dress ensemble, caught Porsche's attention as she gradually made her way amongst the eagerly waiting crowd to the receiving desk, where she quietly observed the chatter before ringing the silver-plated bell positioned directly in front of her. Porsche, in awe of the hostess' ability to command such attention, watched in admiration while making mental notes to herself.

Once the volume lowered, Ginale, the hostess, introduced herself and welcomed those gathered for coming. She gave them a brief history of the winery and included the agenda for the day's self tour before pushing the tablet, safely secured on the Mahogany, star-studded wall behind her. Beyond the wall was a hidden fifteen passenger elevator; destination... The Basement.

Ginale divided guests into proportionate groups and escorted them inside the glass elevator where they were taken underground to the private cellar; a cellar specifically designed for VIP and Elite guests. Walking down the moderately lit, lukewarm corridor, guests marveled at the eccentric African American Painting Collections on the walls, while paying special attention to the rows and rows of three column high, stalked, wooden barrels of wine with engraved platelets classifying the brand, title and year, in jet black, bold lettering.

At the end of the barreled lined walkway, with red wine designated to the left and white to the right, were five circular tables of four, elegantly decorated in black and white with splashes of silver and gold. Around the tables stations of grand stature filled with an assortment of cheese, salami, crackers, and mixed breads for the liking. In addition were: mangos, kiwi, strawberry and other assorted exotic fruits dipped in white crème and black and white chocolate. Dispersed throughout the room were waiters positioned to ensure: glasses remained filled, food remained stalked, and the needs of guests were undeniably met.

Porsche wasted no time at all jumping on the band wagon. She immediately grabbed a plate and stood in line behind a hefty woman, excited to pack her plate with all the gourmet delicacies, even though she had just finished a full breakfast. Scouring the arrangement, Porsche systematically strategized what she was going to eat and how she was going to pile everything on her plate, not caring one inkling about her girlish figure or who may possibly scrutinize her.

"Now this spread looks good," Roger stated as he stood directly behind her in line. Roger was a pro-basketball player from Canada who stood six feet, five inches tall. He had a short fade and slim yet muscular physique with noticeable definitions in his biceps, triceps and calves that protruded outside his black tank top and black and blue, long walking shorts.

Turning around, Porsche smiled with interest as she took a quick scope of his well-trimmed goatee and thick lips. "Yes, I'm especially looking forward to those chocolate strawberries. I can only guess how juicy they must taste." Porsche accented the words "juicy" and "taste" to the ninth degree as she continued looking at Roger, but this time as though the strawberries were the meal and HE was the main dessert.

Sliding his black sunglasses off his eyes and replacing them on top of his head, he smiled widely with a devilish grin deepening his dimples on each side of his toffee colored cheeks. Looking into Porsche's eyes and then surveying downward from the top her neck to the bottom of her toes, he sarcastically replied, while stroking his goatee with his left index finger and thumb, "Yeah, and I'm sure that's not the only thing that's juicy to the taste."

Somewhat embarrassed by Roger's flirtatious innuendos, Porsche still loved it; a man who was testing her at her very own game. For the first time, Porsche had no quick wit response. No, on the contrary, all that was voiced was but a mere uncomfortable giggle while experiencing an overwhelming, sensual feeling of being stimulated with a host of uncontrollable urges yearning to be met.

Eliminating any further eye contact, Porsche quickly turned around to maintain her sense of respectability and to get her Mahogany Vida In Check. She closed her eyes and quietly said to herself Mahogany Vida, Mahogany Vida, Mahogany Vida.

Porsche wasn't ready and didn't want to display any outward signs of vulnerability, at least not yet. No, she had to be the one in control and anything outside of that was not an option.

At this point, the only thing she could think of, in

order to stack the decks back into her favor was to say, in all of her sassiness, "wouldn't you like to know." Smiling in approval, at her better late than never comeback, she turned back around, but this time with the vivaciousness and confidence of a champion; Ha Ha.., she said to herself under her breath, I got my Mahogany Vida in Check! Roger just smiled at her antics leaving him amped up even more to get to know her.

After securing her seat at one of the open tables, Porsche ventured off to the adjoining room just beyond where the food was located. As she walked inside the open doorway, she stood motionless in the center of the room not knowing where to go or what to do. Different tasting stations in sets of two were positioned alongside the entire perimeter of the room and behind them on the mirrored, all inclusive, glass bar were two barrels of red and white wines to analyze, taste and enjoy. In the center, where she stood, were a series of tall round tables for visitors to congregate, network and converse.

Still stationary, Porsche was trying to make up her mind regarding where to go first. As she looked from one station to the next, she noticed Drisco, Yolie's bartender friend, behind the station to the left. But before she could wander over there, she felt someone ease their hand into hers. It was Noah, a familiar face from her night at the bar; her organic man-made breakfast.

"Hello again," Noah said in a deep voice bringing Porsche out of her somewhat comatose state. Porsche looked startled. "Have a drink with me."

Smiling widely, Noah gave her a little nudge and led her to the station next to Drisco where another bartender had four wine glasses lined up and ready to be filled. Once seated, the bartender began his spiel about the wine, asked a series of questions to determine the appropriate choice for each of their pallets, and then began to pour. The mood was romantic and the ambiance breathtaking, especially for an underground winery, but the conversation and companionship left very little to be desired. Porsche had already spent the night with this man, and although fine as hell, and well equipped, she was not trying to go down that road and spend the entire day with him as well. Porsche was moving forward, commitment was the last thing on her mind, and she wasn't trying to be tied down with any one particular man while on vacation.

Sure, they had some drinks, had some laughs, got

there freak on and had a great time, she thought to herself, but today was a new day so why the heck was he all in my space trying to rain on my parade. All Porsche could do was take one of her deep breaths, indicating her pure irritation of him.

Drisco could visually see Porsche wasn't feeling him and felt a duty to rescue her under the circumstances. Smiling at her, he watched as the conversation was minimal, as was the eye contact. Minutes had gone by, what seemed liked eternity when Drisco walked over to her.

"Sorry to interrupt, but I think I promised you a drink?" Looking into Drisco's eyes with the reaction of eternal thankfulness, Porsche quickly nodded in agreement. She was overwhelmed by his kind gesture, as no one had ever rescued her before, not genuinely anyway, and not that she would ever admit to needing to be rescued but just the same, she was thankful. "Excuse us." Drisco, being the gentleman he was, held out his forearm and helped her off the tall barstool. He then escorted her to his station and assisted her onto the stool directly in front of him.

"So, how are you? Seemed like you needed a little

help over there." Drisco barred no cockiness, arrogance or necessitated any kudos for his kind gesture helping a damsel in distress. He was just being himself, helping out a friend.

"I'm good. Uh, thank you for that," Porsche said humbly. Porsche didn't know what to say and wasn't accustomed to men treating her with, well, respect. She was usually the prey to the outside world yet internally and privately, she was the aggressor, the hunter, lock, stock and barrel. She felt she always had to act and look a certain way for others to pay attention. Why, she didn't know. She had been this way for as long as she could remember and this was the first time she felt differently.

"So, where is your partner in crime today?" Drisco scoured the room but didn't see Yolie anywhere.

"Who?" Porsche, still in a state of shock was not hearing let alone listening to anything Drisco was saying. She was completely oblivious to the conversation. "Who are you talking about?" She repeated.

"Yolie?" he said. "Your friend?" Drisco, paying little attention to Porsche's odd behavior began pouring some white wine… an island favorite.

Finally, noticing Porsche's discomfort, he put down

the bottle, leaned forward putting both hands on the edge of the bar, and said with concern in his voice, "Penny for your thoughts?"

It was at that point that Drisco leaned back and removed a shot glass off the back counter placing it in front of her but not before dropping a penny on the counter and turning the empty glass over, directly on top of it. "This one's on the house."

With a questionable, school girl grin, Porsche slanted her head to the side and couldn't help but smile at him. Looking at Drisco in his dark brown eyes, she felt his smile shining through, but all she could muster up to say was, "Nothing. I'm good. Thank you." Porsche picked up the goblet in front of her by the stem, swirled the wine around in her glass, swept it underneath her nose in a rhythmic motion to capture the sweet smell, and then took a small sip. Trying not to make eye contact, she attempted to glance in every other direction while indirectly answering his questions. Feeling a bit uncomfortable, but enjoying Drisco's company, Porsche stood up and thanked him for the wine. Excusing herself, she indicated that she had a plate of food waiting for her but that it was nice seeing him again.

"No problem," Drisco said smiling at her poor attempt of an excuse and uneasiness. "I hope you enjoy the rest of your stay." Porsche gave a half- cocked smile, and with the wine glass in her hand, walked back into the room to sit at her table. Porsche was baffled by her emotions, and unable to analyze the situation in order to calm her nerves. She engulfed the full glass of wine with one quick swallow.

"You must be thirsty." Not realizing she had an audience, Porsche looked up and saw Roger sitting beside her watching her.

Without responding she looked at him in a daze, pointed to his glass and said, "you gonna drink that?" But before Roger could answer, Porsche grabbed his wine and consumed it as though she was suffering from chronic dehydration.

Noticing there was something wrong with Porsche, even after speaking to her briefly in the food line, Roger could tell this was not her personality and she was definitely off her game.

"I don't know what just happened in there, but something is obliviously troubling you." Roger was passionate, concerned and wanted to help. He put his hand over hers on the table and squeezed it, in attempts to comfort her and quietly said, "I know you don't know me but I want to help deter you away from whatever it is that's bothering you. Will you allow me to do that?" Porsche said nothing. All she could do was look down at her plate with a blank slate.

Taking a hold of her chin, he lifted her head until their eyes met and asked in a concerned voice, "okay?" Porsche hesitantly nodded.

Roger motioned to the nearest bartender to give him two more glasses of wine and as he waited he rubbed her back in a circular motion consoling her. Of what, he didn't know and at this point didn't care. Returning with the wine was Drisco. Looking up, Porsche acted like she saw a ghost, and just as soon as the glasses were placed onto of the white linen table, Porsche reached over to grab one, but not before Roger blocked her by putting his hand over the top of the goblet stopping her dead in her tracks.

Thanking Drisco for the wine, Roger was now a little more concerned than before at Porsche's desperate attempt to chug a lug and so was Drisco. Drisco couldn't help but notice Porsche's continued obscure behavior, even for Porsche, and couldn't comprehend the sudden change in her conduct from the night before. As he walked back to the adjoining room, Drisco looked back at Porsche worried yet hoping she would be alright.

"You okay?" Roger inquired still covering the glass with the palm of his hand. Clearing her chest with a shake of her head while re-adjusting herself to sit up straight, Porsche acted as though everything were alright.

"Yeah," Porsche said as if she were trying to convince herself. "I'm fine," she said softly sounding somewhat disconnected. As Porsche looked around the room she knew she had to get herself together. She knew she was neither acting nor feeling like her normal egotistical self. Catching her bearings she caught Rogers's eyes. "What?" she said throwing her hands in the air. "I'm fineeeee."

With more assurance she repeated herself again, this time with the feisty tone, Roger already knew and came to adore, "I'm fine. Of course I'm fine." Porsche ended her decree with a slight chuckle and roll of her eyes. And with that self-doubting statement, she maneuvered the glass away from Roger and took her sip of wine.

"Tell you what," Roger hesitated for a moment. "I have an idea." Roger waited for a second before he continued, leaving Porsche curious as to what Roger had up his sleeve.

With a slight smile and excitement in his voice, Roger said, "come with me." Roger knew exactly what to do. He stood up and walked around the table extending his hand as an open invitation for Porsche to join him.

"Where are we going?" Porsche asked.

"Just follow me," he answered with a grin as he turned his head to direct her away from the public display of onlookers. Roger walked Porsche to a quiet location in the back side of the basement amongst several three story columns' of wine barrels. Leaning against the barrels, with his hands in hers, Roger looked at Porsche but didn't make a sound and Porsche surprisingly didn't utter a word.

Nervous from the dead silence, Porsche began scouring the room as if there was something to see; something she could focus on outside of this adoring, gorgeous man before her who evidently held all the cards. "Okay, so you got me here; now what?" Porsche said anxiously, awaiting some sound, any sound beyond the confines of their own breathe and driblets of babble, heard in the not too far off distant background.

"Sssshhh, Sssshhh, Sssshhh," Roger said repeatedly putting his index finger over her mouth to quiet her rambling. "All in due time. Just close your eyes and relax for a minute." Roger smiled once again but this time with more confidence than before. He knew she was like putty in his hands.

Taking a deep breath, Porsche was frustrated that she had to follow his directions for she know if she didn't, he wouldn't leave her alone. Roger knew Porsche was stubborn from the moment they met and she opened her mouth. Porsche didn't realize he had already been observing her at the bar the night before and caught a glimpse of her as they waited in the lobby. He knew her type all too well.

"Fine, my eyes are closed. Now what?" Porsche's horns were showing and Roger didn't care. He was patient. He was secure. He knew what he was doing. "Well," Porsche sounded more irritated than before.

"Just relax Porsche. I'm right here with you. Can you just be quiet and trust me for a moment." Roger was dominant and took control over the situation leaving Porsche in a state of shock as she shifted her hips to get comfortable from one side to the other, this time folding her arms like a kid having a temper tantrum.

"Trust him," she said to herself. "I don't even know the brother.  How's he going to tell me to be quiet? He's got me all pinned up against this barrel. Who the hell does he think he is?" Porsche was blatantly having an ongoing conversation with herself, cussing him out from here to kingdom come, but out loud, didn't utter a sound. She remained silent.

Roger could see Porsche's wheels spinning in her head due to her jetting eyeballs vividly seen underneath her closed lids and slight transition of her mouth from tense to relaxed and back to tense. Roger watched and waited in silence until he felt Porsche was ready; ready to be open for whatever was going to happen next. Meanwhile, Roger had arranged for the waiters to set up a private setting for two.

"Here sit down." Porsche opened her eyes to find that Roger had arranged a beautiful, romantic table for them beyond the spotlight of any who could see and hear them. "Porsche, I'm going to give you something." Porsche was speechless. She was now being cooperative and silent as she patiently waited.

Roger took a juicy strawberry from the black, china

dish in front of him and leaned forward as he slowly used it to outline the top of her lips moistening them with the driblets of water from the fresh berry. Looking into his eyes, Porsche felt a warm sensation come over her. She wanted so badly to kiss him and partake of this fruit, but as she leaned over to act, Roger teasingly removed his lips from her path and in one fell swoop the strawberry was also gone.

Roger began again but this time with a different berry outlining her bottom lip. And with each try, she waited for him to let her taste. He continued this process with different fruit, some dipped in chocolate and others in crème. With each choice, he randomly selected which ones to soak in wine and which to remain free and unrefined. Randomly he would entice her with a gentle kiss as he fed her, teased her and catered to the passions she was so deserving of. Porsche loved the game, loved the company, and continued to live in the moment in the underground cellar of the basement.

# Timeless

Days had gone by and Yolie was spending a lot of time with Aaron, conversing with Drisco and reminiscing about her forbidden treatment with Jace. Porsche, on the other hand was drifting from one Thoroughbred to the next, dodging Noah, and stealing private moments with Roger. Life was just as it should be... timeless and unpredictable.

Time had seemed to slip on by from one day to the next as Yolie and Porsche enjoyed as many elements as possible on the forbidden island, from river rafting and jungle explorations, to local activities at the resort. But today was like no other; this was the day they had been looking forward too. Today was the day Drisco would take them on a personal island tour to the forbidden twin falls.

The sun hovering above was riveting hot, yet the slight island breeze added comfort and serenity. As Yolie and Porsche hopped into Drisco's 4X4, black jeep wrangler sport, they began their excursion through time as he showed them sections of the island where tours were not permitted to go and the forbidden falls only the natives knew about and were only allowed to enter.

The waterfalls were located deep within the tropical forest hidden from view. There were no paved cobblestones, dirt roads or cemented infrastructures that would lead or guide them to their final destination. No, it lay buried, in the rustics of the jungle, with trees that bared similarity to that of weeping willows, tall bamboo, intertwined grapevines and colorful exotic vegetation.

"Where are we?" Porsche said perplexed looking around as Drisco stopped in the middle of nowhere amongst sacred trees, ivy, creeks and vines. "It looks so… desolate," Porsche whispered under her breath as though she had an awful sour taste in her mouth.

"It looks beautiful," Yolie quickly replied ignoring Porsche's negativity and defending her beautiful surroundings. She hurriedly gathered her things and climbed out of the jeep, intrigued at all the exquisiteness and magnificence around her.

"This way," Drisco said nonchalantly ignoring the little spat between the ladies, as he turned around and led the way through whistling, overgrown tree passages.

"Watch your step," as he straddled over a small hollow oak and helped Yolie jump over a moderately sized creek. The journey was short but the terrain was a tad bit treacherous. Drisco continued to look over his shoulder at Yolie and Porsche making sure they were alright, offering as much assistance as needed. There was minimal conservation on the walk to the forbidden falls as Yolie looked from side to side admiring her surroundings while Porsche bobbed, weaved, ducked, and tip toed around anything that even looked like it could be moving. Ultimately, the quiet journey was to enlist embrace the beauty of nature, the fresh air, and all its exquisiteness on the roadmap to the falls.

Upon reaching their final destination, Drisco stopped short in his tracks, overlooking the mountain, extended his hands widely out in front of him, and loudly belted, "Welcome to the Forbidden Falls." Drisco was excited and honored that he had the opportunity to share this experience with Porsche and Yolie. Looking once again over his shoulder, this time smiling, he asked, "You guys ready to go down?" Yolie and Porsche both nodded eagerly in anticipation as they veered over the hilltop.

"Wow," Yolie said as they arrived at the string of

waterfalls. "I have never seen anything like this before." Mesmerized by the sights, Yolie paused for a brief moment and then exhaled. "This is absolutely stunning." Yolie couldn't believe her eyes as they looked at the series of twin waterfalls, surrounding the perimeters of the half moon shaped cliffs that cascaded into the hot springs, pool of water, below. Yolie had traveled all over the world singing and performing and nothing took her breath away like this.

Porsche's excitement upon arrival of the forbidden falls finally unveiled itself in the midst of her sweet bitterness. She couldn't wait to run her toes through the white sands and dip her body into the warm water where she enviously watched the natives basking in the sun and playing in the springs.

Walking down the steep terrain onto the sandy white beaches below, Drisco was paying special attention to Yolie making sure she didn't lose her footing. Today he was off duty and could communicate what he's been thinking and feeling from the time he first laid eyes on her. Yolie, oblivious didn't pay attention but Porsche, on the other hand noticed and was not impressed as she still couldn't help but jilt her unexpected feelings toward

Drisco in the basement.

Reaching the bottom was like a child entering Disneyland for the first time; it was filled with excitement and anticipation with the inability to make a concrete decision of where to go first. The lagoon was laid with bamboo hideaways for the exotic, bamboo umbrellas for the loungers, and volleyball nets, frisbees and other sport and water toys and equipment for the outdoorsy natives and young at heart.

Yolie didn't want to waste a moment's time as she quickly threw off her sarong, dropped her belongings, and ran off to join one of the volleyball teams. Porsche, on the other hand, had another idea in mind. She was going to make herself real comfortable as she took her stance making sure to catch preying eyes as she slowly unveiled her newest lavender string bikini. As Drisco started to trample off, Porsche swiftly asked Drisco for assistance as she saw him begin to wander off like a lost little puppy dog behind Yolie. Hesitantly he obliged but not without staying focused on Yolie so as to not lose sight of her. He knew he had to get her alone, but when?

Yolie was enjoying the scenery as she played forward, on the team, running, gliding and enjoying the outdoors.

Although the sun was hot, there was a slight breeze offering relief, and with each break, the varying teams would take turns running to the still waters off the sandy beaches only to retake their rightful position against the net. It was 4 and 0 and Yolie's team was ahead but not without the competitiveness of cheap shots, loud talking, and desperate measures to sway the other team to lose their concentration. Yolie was no exception with her loud, trash talking "politically correct" innuendos. She felt comfortable and amongst these strangers she found solitude, friendship and playful competition as she was able to get a few digs in, laughed and congregated amongst her new found friends.

As Yolie continued to play, she found herself constantly distracted by the soothing sounds of the twin falls falling to the side of her; and there she watched, in a daze, as couples playfully jumped from the canvas peak into the rippling waters below while others made out underneath the spray with warm water engulfing every square inch on their bodies. It was only a few moments that had gone by, or so she thought, when she was struck with a sonic pain in her side so intense that it threw her off balance plummeting her down into the sand hitting the grain like a shovel digging for gold. Grabbing her side, she screamed as the pain shot up and down her leg and spine and it wasn't long before onlookers gathered around her hoping and praying that she would be alright.

"Are you alright," a young man said as he rushed to her side filled with anxiety and genuine concern. Rocking in the motion of the pain, all Yolie could say was that it hurt while grabbing her side with tears trickling down her sun beat face. "Here, I got you." The young man gently picked her up off the sand, and carried her away as on lookers opened a vented path for him to carry her through to one of the bamboo hideaways, away from the heat, the embarrassment, spirited teammates and noisy beach settlers.

Drisco, seeing all the commotion ran over to Yolie, trampling over his own feet as though he couldn't get there fast enough with Porsche scurrying closely behind. By the time he had got there, Yolie was already vanished; one with no traces left behind. The volleyball game continued and new members had already taken her place. Worried, Drisco began to comb the area asking questions but receiving little to no results. He finally found someone who was willing to tell him of her volleyball accident and injury to her side leaving a bruise that was easily identifiable to the human eye. The only thing they had no knowledge of was her whereabouts.

On the backside of the falls, Yolie was being well taken care of with ice, healing rocks, beverages and unadulterated VIP treatment. "How are you feeling now," the young man said concerned, hoping his special concoctions and home remedy's healed away at least the burning pain. Yolie's excruciating pain definitely was minimized but Yolie was still in a daze between the strike of the ball and all of the various blends and ole' school island mixtures.

Feeling a little bit better she tried to sit up but couldn't. Her strength and energy were just not there. Trying to sit up she realized she wasn't 100% and the frustration set in. Yolie was determined not to let the day go by and miss everything; not when she wouldn't have anything to show for it but a few bruised ribs.

Sucking it up, Yolie said, "better, thank you," as she smiled and looked up at this 6 foot 3 inch, well stocked man in his low rise trunks. The crevices of his manliness highlighted the very pathway to his endowment causing inquiring minds to wonder just where his well-defined hips and lower extremity lines ultimately linked, under his semi-wet, swim shorts.

Trying again, this time she beckoned for his assistance. "Can you please help me…," Yolie stuttered fishing for his name yet nothing came to mind as she focused on her footing struggling to sit up with the ultimate goal of standing.

"Uh, maybe you should just sit a little while longer," the young man said with uneasiness in his voice and slight smirk on his face as he watched Yolie fumble trying not to lose her footing. Taking a deep breath and shaking his head in annoyance, at Yolie who refused to listen, he slowly clawed the front of his hair while lifting his long, dark brown dreads out of his way, away from his face. As he positioned them just behind his right ear, Yolie could see his biceps and triceps going to work grabbing her attention; that was until he swooped and dropped them down his back in preparation to assist her.

"No! I'm here on this beautiful island, by these unbelievable falls and I am not going to miss this once in a lifetime experience because of my stupid ribs." Frustrated, Yolie sighed. She began to get even more aggravated as she thought of all the time wasted, away from the fun and the springs, due to this freak accident. Looking up with tears in her eyes, Yolie pleaded, once again stumbling to find his name, "Please, I don't want to miss this..."

Cutting her off in mid sentence he responded. "Jace. My name is Jace." And with a smile of contentment and a cool and calm demeanor, Jace carefully leaned forward to offer Yolie balance and support as he assisted her into a sitting position. It was at that moment that all of Yolie's concentration swiftly shifted from any attempts to reconcile her mood and energy to the words he just uttered. Stunned, Yolie's mind started working a mile a minute and with each moment that passed, her mind was consumed with memories of his hands, his strength, his hand written note, and the possibility of whether this indeed was the same Jace that provided her forbidden spa treatment. Was this the Jace she fantasized about, she wondered. What if...

Taking a deep breath followed by a clearing of her throat, she knew she had to get her Mahogany Vida in check and not display any inclination as to any illicit thoughts and inquires that were running so wildly around in her head. "Did you just say Jace?" Yolie anxiously waited for an answer as her mind continued to spin, shifting from one of surprise to the other of awkwardness, and then to pure unadulterated fantasy. But, before he could respond, Yolie instantaneously had another question blurting out of her mouth. "Uh, by any chance do you work at the resort up the road in the day spa?" Not knowing if she really wanted the answer to her loaded question, she continued to wait in anticipation as her heart began to skip beats not normal let alone conceivable.

Reading her eyes and listening to her body language, Jace smiled with a devilish grin, and answered "yes," in an undertone only he really knew the meaning of. Jace had thoughts himself but mainly about the small intricacies of Yolie's own personal, forbidden, unveiling and all the emotions he tried so desperately to conceal beyond the mask that she wore.

Did he just say yes? Yolie's mind soared like an American Eagle flying down to capture her prey. Yes, she said again to herself as a series of sensations flooded every inkling of her being tapping into her very existence as a woman. Those three little letters Y E S were more powerful than ever imaginable.  YES!

Looking into Jace's eyes, it was evident he could read

her thoughts and Yolie could read his. He continued to assess her nonverbal communication and Yolie was definitely speaking loud and clear for both of them. The intensity was strong and the energy magnetic and nothing or no one could tear their stronghold apart. Jace knew in his heart that he would see her again following the forbidden treatment. When, he didn't know but only felt.

Leaning in, Jace gently touched the side of her face with the back of his big hands and as he continued to look deep into her eyes, Yolie completely forgot about the pain or any life outside of the bungalow drapes.

The sun was going down and the warm late afternoon breeze was showing itself against the white linen drapes connected by thick intertwined bamboo layers. The sunset was evident, preying off the distant cliffs and colorizing the water as it hit the surface of the streams below. Moving toward each other to seal the deal, Yolie and Jace were in complete agreement and just as their lips were about to touch, it was mildly interrupted.

"There you are. We've been looking all over for you," Drisco said with a grin on his face knowing he had just interrupted something. Although the interruption took place, Yolie and Jace's eyes continued to be fixated on each other, unable to pry away even for an inkling of a second.

"Uh, I think we're interrupting something," Porsche said hesitantly yet smiling that they just walked into something that Drisco was definitely not expecting. "Maybe, we should… go," she said looking at Drisco, gesturing toward the door in an over exaggerated motion. Turning back she looked at Yolie giving her a slight wink of the eye and said, "We'll see you later. Oh, and glad you're okay." Porsche again tried to pivot to leave the room, but this time with a point of the finger and forward movement toward the exit, in attempts to have Drisco follow her as she backed out the bungalow corridor, but Drisco wasn't having it; at least not without Yolie.

"Yolie, are you okay? What happened? Are you ready for me to take you back?" Drisco started asking questions a mile a minute then anxiously awaited a response but time was not on his side. He wanted New York speed and what he got was laid-back Southern Comfort.

Slowly looking away from Jace and catching the eyes of Porsche, Yolie responded with a fatigued tone in her voice as though she had not a care in the world. "I'm fine Drisco, thanks for asking. Jace has been taking good care of me." Shifting her focus back to Jace, she smiled as she took his hand in hers and squeezed it tightly.

Unresponsive to Yolie's nonverbal communication and blatant disregard of her auditory words, Drisco reacted as though it were imminent that he should take her back to the resort due to her traumatic ordeal. Reading Yolie's animated facial expressions, Porsche voluntarily stepped into the conversation and offered Jace's assistance to return Yolie to her room back safely. Nodding, Jace confirmed Porsche's announcement and with confidence and sarcasm in his voice he responded "of course," with a bellowing smile.

Drisco continued to try and hold a conversation with Yolie, but it was evident that Yolie didn't want to be bothered and wanted to be left alone. She was tired, in pain, and a tad bit dehydrated and all she wanted was to relax and watch the sunset as Jace held her in his strong, athletic arms; nothing more, nothing less.

"Come on Drisco, let's go. It's late. I'm ready to go back to the resort." Porsche tugged on the side of Drisco's shirt, but he didn't budge. "Yolie's fine. We'll see her when she gets back." Still, there was no response. Irritated that Drisco was all of the sudden obsessed with Yolie;

Porsche couldn't help but stand in the doorway with her arms crossed and lips poked out. Her attitude was on the rise and, like a box of lemon drops, the sourness of it all was apparent and overwhelming. She was not pleased, in the slightest, that more attention was being paid to Yolie than her. Although it was not a competition between the two, she was feeling neglected and wanted some of that testosterone spotlight on her. Porsche just couldn't understand what the heck was going on. I mean, who wouldn't want all of this, she thought to herself.

Watching Porsche have her little pity party, Drisco suddenly began to feel a little guilty by his insensitivity and behavior. He uttered a few more words to Yolie and then grabbed Porsche's hand and headed silently toward the jeep. Porsche didn't mind the silence, as she was just jazzed that Drisco took her hand as though he were open and willing versus the dreaded alternative which was shame by association. However she "won," she didn't care, for all she knew was that the remainder of the evening was theirs, at least from her point of view.

# New Beginnings

That evening highlighted remarkable new beginnings for Yolie and Jace, Porsche and Drisco. Romance for Yolie and Jace was alive and present and anyone who was within close proximity could feel and see the intensity between them. As they held each other that beautiful, sweet, sunset evening, a new connection was made. Simple nibbles on the ear, tender kisses on the lips, and gently massages on the shoulders were but a mere appetizer to the upcoming main course.

Porsche and Drisco, on the other hand, were on a whole other level. And while Yolie and Jace were experiencing passion at the falls, Porsche was busy being preoccupied with creating problematic episodes and questionable scenarios to aid in the facilitation of some sexual unleashing in Drisco. It was quite a trek back to the jeep; especially during the early evening hours when their view was skewed and undermined by the colorful sunset reflections of red, purple, orange and yellow hitting the rocky hills, still waters, and earthly vegetation. Porsche did everything she could think of to harbor any and all of Drisco's attention.

Grabbing hold of Porsche's hand, Drisco helped Porsche over the more treacherous, rugged terrain as it was seemingly more difficult visually to identify where to step safely than it was during those peak morning hours. Being more cognizant of his surroundings, Drisco couldn't help but shift his attention to her, especially when they embarked on a creek that had somehow became more fluid and widespread than when they had crossed it earlier that day.

"What are we going to do?" Looking at the rapid flow of water, Porsche was genuinely concerned and scared for the first time. It was evident by the look of trepidation in her eyes and the sound of uneasiness in her voice that she had an unsettling feeling in her gut; one that was completely unshaven and had unmistakably, rattled her deeply. She already wasn't the outdoorsy type and trying to jump this creek was a hurdle beyond measure, and not exactly within her safety perimeters.

Drisco stood there quietly for a moment assessing the situation, analyzing potential strategies, hoping to create some sort of an action plan for the challenge set before him. Without further contemplation and notice, he picked Porsche up, cradling her like a new born baby against his chest, and instructed her to hold on tight. With a slight scream from being startled by Drisco's spontaneous actions, she unconsciously grabbed him tightly around his neck intertwining her fingers to an iron-clad, locked position thereby decreasing any potential malfunction that could possibly happen if she weren't securely fastened.

Once the initial shock was eliminated, that she was off the ground and safe in his arms, an angelic ray of light shone across her beaming face in approval. Staring at him, attempting to bypass the sunset's glare, she gleamed as she gaped into his light brown eyes; one emotion of satisfaction and the other of fear but the previous sentiment overrode the latter at that moment.

Looking around her, she finally felt protected and at peace. Nothing was going to ruin this; not even Yolie. This was it, she said to herself, as she bit her bottom lip and curled in a little more toward his fit body; just to get closer to him.

As Drisco started across the creek, apprehension once again set in but this time it was different. This time it was somewhat controlled as Porsche buried her head inside his broad chest refusing to peek out into the light.  Feeling Porsche's anxiety, Drisco held her a little bit tighter adding a calming remedy to her nervous state.

"Don't worry, I got you. I'm not going to let you fall." And, as he stumbled across the creek a few times, to some extent losing his balance, his reassurance was in his tender words and upper body strength; for every time Drisco's balance was compromised, he assured her with a tighter grasp, and a consoling kiss on the back of her head that everything was going to be alright. Some of Drisco's steps were uncertain as to whether they were going to successfully transition across without feeling the wrath of nature's disharmony and for that, Porsche shed some tears. Tears not induced by not trusting him but that of fright and panic that mother nature would prevail, and they would both endure a fraction of the earth's wet surface below if they did indeed go plummeting down due to the unsteady, racing, river current.

Drisco tried to keep his composure attempting not to leave any window of opportunity for Porsche to identify any fear or doubt within him as he methodically, cautiously, and carefully crossed the tides as though he were an award-winning gymnast displaying perfect control and that of utter confidence on the balance beam.

It wasn't until they reached the other side when Drisco lost his footing. One – as the unsteady rock was stepped on, it sauntered roughly back and forth like a seesaw at the local community park. Two – Drisco struggled to maintain his balance as he stumbled back and forth, including sideways, just to gain some type of leverage between him and the formidable ground while using Porsche as a equilibrium device, indirectly. Three – the title of champion was announced and Drisco caught the short end of the stick.

Falling to the ground, fear set in as to what type of pain they would endure. Were they going to hit their head on a rock, a stick, or descend straight into the moistened shrubby caused by the evening dew? This time they were lucky. Drisco was able to use his body strength to turn the tides on a bleak situation. He was able to maneuver both of their bodies so he would be the one to feel the brunt of the collapse versus Porsche who would be coddled and cushioned as she fell directly on top of him; eye to eye and mouth to mouth.

Once on the ground, and undeniably safe out of harm's way, the two found a new common denominator that they would ultimately bring them closer together. Looking intensely into each other's eyes while clinging together in each other's arms, for the first time, Drisco saw Porsche in a whole new light. However indescribable, the feeling of comfort and protection set in as well as that of undue respect, as their interest instantaneously grew that sunset evening, toward one another.

What had started off as a bitter sweet day ended in a conglomerate of intense animal magnetism. Simultaneously, Porsche and Drisco began kissing each other, rolling in the dirt, sweeping limbs and body parts uncontrollably from one direction to the other. The only words that sounded were that of groans and moans from the erotic delivery of services. Drisco knew if he wanted this intimacy to continue, he had to do whatever was necessary to protect Porsche's hair at all costs. And that he did, as he ensured that one hand was always used as a shield and cover; for if and when she was ever on the bottom, at the receiving end of his pleasure points.

Porsche was so aroused that she didn't care about her hair; all she yearned for was this rock of a man in front of her. Flipping around on top of him, Porsche straddled his waist and removed her cover up. Leaning forward, she stuck her bottom out, arching her backside and with every moment, whether it was to kiss his neck, his shoulders, or his lips, she could feel him growing and pulsating under his swim trunks. Leaving little to his imagination, Drisco could feel her melon opening, inside her string bikini bottoms, as she grinded her lower extremities, in a circular motion, while peacefully resting on top of him.

"Wait baby, wait a minute," Drisco caringly said with a slight chuckle, trying to catch his breath.

"Uh uh," Porsche said refusing to stop or let him up for even a small breath of fresh air. This is exactly what she had been waiting for and he wanted her to stop now, she thought to herself, huh, I don't think so.

"No, really baby. Let me get the blanket out," Drisco responded as he continued to turn his head from side to side, this time bringing both lips in as though he had dentures and they were just removed. He did this hoping it would disrupt Porsche's flow but at the same time enabling him to get a few more words out without his life being sucked out of him. "Let's get comfortable," he said finally able to spit out those few three short words.

Huffing, Porsche threw back her hands as she relieved

Drisco of his fulfillment duties, praying all the sexual advances would continue and that Drisco wouldn't lose momentum from this slight interruption.

"Here, let me have the blanket." Straightening out her bikini bottoms with the tips of her fingers, Porsche could feel the wetness inside of her and was ready to get pleased even more. She hoped that the brush of evening air wouldn't loom in too quickly and that it would take its time in drying her out.

Flattening the blanket out over the granulated dirt, away from anything that could poke or prod them, Drisco knew exactly what he was doing. The location was private and secure, the weather was lukewarm, and the stars were shining bright. Standing up, further insuring all four corners were ironed out and crinkles and ripples removed, as though he were doing a marine bed check, Drisco extended his hand out to Porsche. Porsche, with a smile on her face and sparkles in her eyes couldn't help but feel tingly and excited as she stepped on the blanket that was made just for her.

Instantaneously, Porsche and Drisco picked up from where they left off sucking, biting, and clawing. Like two carnivores, they demanded each other's attention in ways other humans would not dare to seek. Taking their interactive activity down to the blanket, they rolled around as if they were two little kids at vengeful play and only one could, and would, win. Romance and seduction weren't the words to describe them that evening. It was pure animal magnetism. And, as they threw off and flung each other's bathing suits into the air, they engaged in positions not known to escape beyond the compounds of a bedroom. They didn't care about anything or anyone.

On the other side of the falls, Yolie and Jace were the epitome of passion and romance. Watching the sun go down, Jace began to massage the back of Yolie's neck while gently kissing her shoulders, upper back and lower neckline. And, with the sunset peering into the room, the need of candles for ambiance would've just been an added affect.

Yolie couldn't help but get into the mood as she silently watched the beautiful sunset, sporadically closing her eyes as she leaned slowly to the side giving Jace even more access to nibble on her neck. And as he came around her back to face her, he kissed her on the forehead avoiding the lips but continued in all the other surrounding facial locations; the cheeks, the nose, and the eyes. Yolie was waiting for his lips to touch hers, even if it was just a graze, but it wasn't time; at least not yet. She had to wait a little while longer. Jace was on a path to satisfy Yolie by and all means. Seducing her and creating the mood that only he knew she would enjoy.

"Here, why don't you lay back down and let me finish giving you your massage." Yolie didn't hesitate, question or respond. She immediately accepted with a quick nod and smiled with a keyed up grin as she lay back down but this time on the oversized, circular, plush, flat bed. Smiling with a devilish smirk, Jace loved her quick response and as he positioned her accordingly, on her stomach, he tenderly rubbed his hands over her back and there she eagerly waited for phase two of her forbidden treatment.

Lifting her head up to peer back at him, she said in a sassy tone, "do the same rules apply?"

Jace couldn't help but smile once again as he shook his head at her question. And with a slight snicker, he said "shhhh, you talk too much." Jace took the palm of his hand and gently pushed her head back down upon the padded cushion hoping that would keep her quiet while insinuating to her to enjoy the ride and just relax. All

Yolie could do was chuckle enabling her bottom and stomach to go up and down stimulating Jace's stretch of gravity even further. Stretching out her limbs on each side of her and opening her legs in preparation for entry, Yolie sounded off a big sigh of stillness indicating she was ready, willing and able for whatever was to going to happen next.

And then it happened; the entry into her moistened walls of glory. It was slow; it was sensual; it was erotic yet breathtaking and neither wanted their amazingly grandeur flight of incredible emotions to end. The evening was long, the expectation right on point, and the sensation unbelievably remarkable and passionate. Jace knew just how Yolie wanted to be touched, caressed, and embedded for pure, unadulterated, romantic delight.

# The Day After

The morning after took on a whole new meaning for Porsche, Drisco, Yolie and Jace. They had now returned to the resort but things were different and although it was an experience that would always be remembered and never forgotten, confusion and a tad bit of uncertainty were now added into the equation. The falls left a lasting effect that no one could question and there would always be that "forbidden" bond that would bind them forever.

Upon return, both Yolie and Porsche slept half the day away in their individual suites while Jace and Drisco returned to work early that morning. Waking up Yolie felt different; feelings she couldn't quite put her finger on. All she knew was that she woke up with a smile on her face, felt a type of happiness and joy she hadn't felt in a very long time and was inspired to write, to sing, and rejoice out loud. The only downfall was the explicit rules of the island. She was not to work under any circumstances! But, was writing her heart felt feelings of this magnitude really work? She wanted to write, had a desire to sing, and wanted to shout at the top of her lungs how excited she was even though she wouldn't be able to completely express the unforgettable experience nor the volume of emotions she was feeling and why. Truthfully, who was there she could really tell not to mention who would honestly care. All she knew was that she had this newfound energy that was abundantly overflowing; just yearning to get out.

Getting dressed for a late lunch, Yolie couldn't help the giddiness she felt inside. But, not too soon after, her emotions quickly shifted and the tides were turned for the worse as she began to question the authenticity and reality of it all.

Was this a one night stand? Did Jace feel the same way?

Was she another notch in his belt? Did it mean anything?

And as these negative thoughts came pouring in from the depths of all her insecurities; the same emotions she felt beyond the spotlight when she wasn't performing and was off stage, she thought about the potential of at least one of these questions potentially being unequivocally true and loosely answered with a dumbfounding, "yes."

Slowly, she started feeling herself slip into an aftermath of disappointment peering into isolation nearly veering on seclusion, but for what? A boy? I don't think so! Her unconscious mind finally caught up with her conscious and decided to speak up. No sooner did she feel her body language and mind slip into a listless state when she shifted her mind to the joy that the evening had brought her.

Smiling once again, as she peered at her image in the bathroom mirror, she said sarcastically out loud to her mirrored image, "well… if it was, it sure was good!" Laughing at her abbreviated version of self worth and confidence, she continued to look in the mirror, as her views sporadically shifted from one extreme to the next. It was then that she knew it was time for her to get her Mahogany Vida in Check and stop trippin'. No one was going to ruin this wonderful experience for her, especially not her own self limiting beliefs. She knew, deep within that she deserved this happiness and no one or nothing, including her own lack of confidence and insecurity, was going to take that joy away.

Knowing she needed to pull herself together from the slight funk she was temporarily in, she knew one instantaneous way to accomplish such a task was to turn on some sounds and rev up the volume. Once that happened, Yolie's vibe shifted and she began to once again embrace her Mahogany Vida as she danced from one room to the next listening to the locals' calypso, reggaetone music.

Porsche in the adjacent suite was two minutes away from hitting the lobby floor and gracing the foyer with her presence. She had just hung up the phone with Yolie letting her know to be ready when she got there or she would meet her at their regular location downstairs, at the café, in front of the sliding glass doors.

Yolie wasn't trying to rush. Yes, she was hungry but she was quite content with the tempo of her actions. She was putting the finishing touches of makeup on her face when she heard the loud knock on the door.

"Hold on a sec," Yolie shouted from inside the bathroom. She knew if she didn't answer or respond Porsche would make all kinds of commotion in the open corridor. Taking a sigh of relief, to add calmness to her state of mind, she added a few more stokes with her lip liner brush to blend in her gloss, lip stick and liner, to complete the final touches. There were only a few more strokes left to be finished when the knock sounded again but this time a little more forcefully.

Frustrated, Yolie threw the bronze colored liner brush down inside her makeup bag and headed to the door. Mumbling under her breath, as she fixed her dress, she said in a controlled tone to herself, "this girl can't wait for anything, dang." And with that thought, she turned the knob and opened the door.

"Hey!" "Where have you been?" Standing in the doorway unannounced and uninvited was Aaron looking dashing and debonair as always.

"Uh... Huh?" Yolie, caught off guard, was definitively speechless as she stood complacent like a marked target. She wasn't expecting to see Aaron standing there in her entryway and certainly hadn't had time to process everything that had occurred over the past twenty-four hours. She knew she hadn't had the opportunity to see or talk to him since she left early yesterday morning for the falls as everything happened so fast and there was just no time. The plan was to hang out with her girl and take an innocent, pleasurable excursion, around the island; take some photos; and return by late lunch, early dinner.

What do I say? What can I say? She thought to herself. Do I explain but explain what? What is there to explain? Yolie was stumbling for words with an obscene amount of guilt, ambivalence, and uncertainty. Why? She didn't know. It wasn't like she was committed or anything. Yet, the feelings remained.

Repeating his words again but this time in a more direct yet non- threatening manner, Aaron looked directly into Yolie's eyes, bordering on informal interrogation and said, "Where've you been? I've been looking for you everywhere."

Just before Yolie could answer, Porsche approached from behind wedging herself between Yolie, Aaron and the open doorway. "Oh, heeeyyy." Porsche said, surprised to see Aaron standing there. "You're up HERE kinda early," she said in a questionable egotistical tone. Aaron wasn't trying to engage Porsche and her antics today. Between Yolie's unusual behavior and Porsche's conduct, Aaron could tell something was up but wasn't sure what. "You trying to get you some," Porsche said smiling, amused at herself.

"Porsche," Yolie scolded, embarrassed but not surprised those words came out of her mouth.

"Excuse me," Aaron said, slighted offended at Porsche's insinuation.

"What? What'd I say?" Pausing for a brief moment as she stared at Yolie and Aaron's shocked face displaying utter disgust and disbelief, Porsche illustrated no signs of regret. Without forethought or taking another second to reflect on what she just said, she continued "ya'll need to get some booty or something. Ya'll too wound up around here." And with that said, Porsche placed her hands on her hips, smiled and shook her head from side to side.

"Porsche, would you stop," Yolie said irritated that she was only adding more fuel to the fire and not helping the already uncomfortable situation.

Looking at Yolie's face, Porsche could tell she was uneasy, uncomfortable and nervous. Realizing this was more serious to Yolie then she had realized, Porsche took a few steps back to recuperate her stance and then said, "dang, I'm just kidding Yolie. Lighten up." Shaking her head, as if to say "really, are you serious," Porsche knew she had to do something. This was way too serious for her, unnecessary, and a bit ridiculous.

Without further notice, Porsche grabbed Yolie's hand and pulled her outside the door. And with one last tug,

Porsche commented, "common' we got to go." Stumbling over her feet as Porsche pulled, Yolie only had enough time to close the door behind her and tell Aaron she was sorry and that she'd catch up with him later.

Startled, Aaron just stood there still, like a porcelain statue, in complete and utter dismay at what just happened. At first, he didn't move an inkling but then turned and watched astonishingly as Yolie and Porsche stepped into the elevator. And there he stood, observing quietly until the steel doors closed tightly behind them.

In the elevator, Yolie gave Porsche the riot act regarding her disrespect, ruthlessness and the ghettoish candor she displayed upstairs. But after all that was said and done, she thanked Porsche for getting her out of that situation with Aaron even though she didn't approve of her less than desirable methods.

"Girl, you know I got you," was all that Porsche said as she nudged Yolie in the arm and smiled trying to shed some light on a less than desirable situation.

And with a half smile and a roll of the eyes, Yolie responded, "yeah, I know."

# Mixing It Up

Once in the lobby, Porsche was trying to do her own thing. She was ready to settle the savages but in the back of her mind, she was really hoping to run into Drisco. A quick lunch at the café, and then Yolie and Porsche parted ways for a late dinner that evening before heading to the airport to go back home.

Yolie felt like she needed some reprieve from the morning dilemma with Aaron so she sought out to the forbidden spa hoping to catch up with Jace.

Porsche on the other hand, headed to the pool hoping to find Drisco in his stark white shorts that showed off his well defined, thick calves. What she was hoping for she didn't know. She just wanted to see him, if nothing else.

Walking out to the pool, Porsche started having an uneasy feeling in her stomach. Trying to pay no attention and thinking it may have to do with something she ate at the café, she continued to walk along the embankment of the large pool until she settled upon the private cabana area where she first saw Drisco serving drinks to Yolie and Aaron. As she approached, she couldn't help but shake the uncomfortable feeling she was being watched. And she was right. For adjacent to her, sitting at the bar, by the private pool, was Roger, Noah and Kem drawn to her every step and every move.

There was nothing she could do and no where she could hide at this moment. They had already seen her and had been watching her for heavens knows how long. Forming a fake smile to get her through this prickly situation, she mumbled to herself, "what the… why the heck are they all here and how in the world do they all know each other." With game face on, Porsche approached confident not showing a morsel of trepidation about this awkward situation.

"Hey guys," Porsche said, veering into each of their eyes as though she were giving each of them her undivided attention.

"Hello yourself," Roger replied looking at Porsche as though he were ready to engulf her if only she were served on a platter and doused with an insurmountable amount of whipped crème.

"Common' and join us," Kem said smiling as he got up and placed an empty stool between he and Roger hoping this time to get some equal playing time.

Clearing her throat, as she performed a quick surveillance of her surroundings with her eyes, Porsche agreed for there was no sign of Drisco in sight. Taking a deep breath she relaxed a little bit enabling her to get into her Diva Zone. "So, what are you boys up to?" Porsche was quick to turn the focus back on them as she appeared anxious yet extraordinarily overconfident displaying all forms of sexiness and sensuality in her high intensity pink, short summer dress. From the over pouring exhibit of her cleavage to her sultry, well oiled thighs and legs, Porsche was ready for the summer breeze to graze on by facilitating the instant, non-coerced uplift of her dress. A raise just enough to peek from underneath where the sun didn't shine but would allow others, focusing on the male species, to see her in all her morning glory.

"Oh, just hanging out, having a few drinks, and talking," Noah replied as he gave her a wink with his all showing thirty-two teeth glaring smile. Porsche didn't like the possible innuendo from where that wink originated and hoped it had nothing to do with her. But, at this point she didn't care. The guys were already ordering drinks for her and as she began hatching them back, nothing seemed to bother her; nothing in the slightest. Words were spilling off her tongue and laughter was mutually shared amongst the drunken trio. Porsche on the other hand was severely tipsy bordering on intoxicated delight.

Continuing to make herself comfortable on the stool, Aaron approached inquiring as to the whereabouts of Yolie. Porsche had a difficult time responding at first as she was filled with laughter, watering eyes, and tequila. She responded flailing her arms in no particular direction, "spa… yeah I think the spa." And with that, she took another shot and continued laughing. Aaron couldn't believe his eyes. Never had he seen Porsche act like this and although she wasn't stinking drunk, she was still out of character, even for Porsche.

"Uh, you okay," Aaron asked genuinely concerned.

"Okay… of course. Of course, I'm okay... hey, you want to join us? Kem, Noah, Roger, this is uh… uhh.. Aaron. This is Aaron. Get Aaron a seat." Porsche was blitzed out of her mind but a lot of it was also good acting. She loved the attention, thrived off the attention and most of all, it was taking her mind off Drisco.

"Hey man, you're welcome to join us," Roger said laughing hysterically.

Disgusted, Aaron said, "no man, I'm good.  Just take care of her okay and don't let her drink anymore. She's a friend of mine." And with that said, Aaron left to find Yolie. Drisco had been observing all of this commotion from a far and wasn't pleased himself at Porsche's behavior, her male companions nor Aaron for leaving her like that. He was so compelled to walk away but it wasn't in his nature; especially, not after all that has happened and all that they've been through. Walking over, Drisco felt disappointed, hurt and a tad bit angry that Porsche allowed herself to get in this inebriated state not to mention her inappropriate outwardly flirtatious behavior.

"Hey Porsche," Drisco said as he approached her from behind. Drisco was not smiling and showed no signs of being pleased with her inappropriate public display of sexual conversation or performance.

"Hi. Hi. Uhhh... Hi Drisco." Upon mere sight of seeing Drisco, and hearing his baritone voice, Porsche immediately got the hiccups which weren't exactly sexy especially when mixed with alcohol and the day's brunch. After being startled, Porsche tried everything she could to look and act guiltless but the damage was already done. She couldn't help the slurring of her words and the glazed look in her eyes no matter how hard she tried. There was no way this afternoon that she was going to look or act innocent.

Drisco stood still, staring at Porsche, as she tried to pull herself together and watched her male companions continuing to laugh, drink and have a good time. And although he was aware of Porsche's exotic and sometimes scrupulous behavior, this wasn't even normal or appropriate, even for her. Drisco wasn't impressed in the slightest and remembered the encounter that he had with each one of them before, from serving them drinks at the night club to the cellar in the basement.

"Can you excuse us for a moment," and with that said, Drisco took Porsche's hand, and helped her off the stool. Porsche didn't realize how intoxicated she actually was until she stood up. Instantly, the blood rushed, the room spun, and all she could do was to grab on to Drisco before her body hit the pavement by the pool.

"Ah man, why you got to take her. We were having a good time over here," Kem said. He was not happy, with Drisco coming in and taking over, but was also too drunk to care. And from that, not another word was spoken.

"Whoa, I don't feel so good," Porsche said as her feet

stood on the lukewarm concrete.

"Yeah, I'm sure you don't," Drisco replied as he once again lifted her up and carried her to the elevator, back up to her suite to lay down. Once in the suite, Drisco carefully laid her across the bed and took off her shoes. He made her take some aspirin with a large glass of water and just sat with her for a moment until she fell asleep.

Watching her in this state shed some new light on their situation. He realized that although they had a great time, she was not the type of girl he could or would be with. And although this was her last night on the island, he would rather remember the positive experience they shared at the falls. Regardless of how they connected, because of that one night, the bond they shared would always be cherished. His heart, for some odd reason though was still with Yolie. Yolie was vastly different than Porsche; sophisticated, confident, adventurous, poised, articulate and beautifully talented. And with that in mind, he left Porsche with a soft kiss to her forehead hoping she would feel better soon.

Yolie was already at the spa waiting in the lounge for Jace to finish with his last client when Aaron walked in. Stunned, Yolie stood straight up questioning what was he doing there. As he began to explain that he didn't like how things ended back at her suite, Jace walked in hearing the last few words of their conversation.

"Hey baby, they told me you were here. Are you ready?" Jace looked confident even though Yolie didn't say a word. She just stood there in silence hoping Porsche would rudely interrupt again. This was her cue. Where the heck was she? What was she waiting for?

Aaron confused looked at Jace and then in slow shutter speed motion glanced back at Yolie. "Hi, I'm Jace." Jace wasted no time for introductions.

"Hey, I'm Aaron." Still no answer, no reply, not even a sound was vocalized from Yolie. It wasn't that she didn't want to respond, she just didn't know how or what to say as of yet. She was confused herself. And as the formalities went under way, Yolie felt confident she could try and make some sense of it all.

Looking at both of them standing there waiting for an explanation from her, she felt like she owed it to them and justifiably to herself. So, as she took a deep breath, she asked if they could all go outside to talk privately and there she began to pour her heart out on her sleeve and explain the scenario of how they each met from beginning to end. What made sense to her, left Aaron speechless and as she began to tie up loose ends with her summarized version of her journey she asked if she could meet them both later so she could have time to think. Aaron said nothing. He just walked away in silence. Jace stood there and once Aaron was out of their sight, he clutched her hand and led her to a beautifully concealed room in the back of the spa.

Jace said nothing as he led her to a plush black circular spa bed in the middle of the room. As he sat her down, he lifted her chin up to kiss his lips, and he led her in the only direction he knew how. He understood her internal struggles and wanted to make things a little easier, less intrusive. If she followed, he would continue but if she drew back, he would retreat and willingly let her go.

As he began to take off her clothes, one article at a time, she closed her eyes and allowed him to do whatever was humanly possible to make any and all insecure feelings go away. From the top of her head down to her toes, he satisfied every morsel of need she ever yearned for or desired. She allowed him to have his way with her and, in the end, they were joined as one. After laying for awhile in the center of her forbidden fruit, he slowly got up and led her to an outside vestibule within the accompanying room where they christened the aroma therapeutic waters of an indoor hot springs Jacuzzi tub.

It was at that moment that it all made sense. It was not Aaron that she saw in her dream that ended as soon as it started, it was Jace. He was the one who she poured her internal feelings and outward emotions too. The one who knew how to touch her in ways no else could imagine. It's who she thought of from the morning of her forbidden treatment to the time at the forbidden falls to the over-sensuous sensations right here, right now. As the evening drew to a close, she knew she had to meet Porsche and get ready to leave, but she wasn't ready. Not yet. Not when she just found him. She wanted to do something special; something she could give him in return for him helping her find herself. But what?

As Yolie left that evening, she made him a promise to meet with her later that evening after dinner in the lounge. Agreeing, Jace smiled with a certainty that everything was going to be okay and off she went to find Porsche.

# The Best of Worlds

Porsche was already up and still light headed from her afternoon party by the pool. She had just finished packing when Yolie entered her suite as though she were on a mission. Without trying to engage in a mix of words, she left a sheet of paper on Porsche's coffee table, filled with a list of actions items for her to complete and then verbally instructed Porsche to be ready after dinner. The plan was to take the red eye flight home. Without waiting for a reply, Yolie left and returned to her suite to pack and prepare for what was going to be their last night on the island.

Following dinner, Yolie and Porsche entered the lounge dressed to impress, as always. All the tables were already occupied and as the waiter led the way to their table for four, Jace and Roger were already there waiting for them. Smiling apologetically, due her previous behavior, Porsche looked at Yolie and then Roger and as they reached their table, Roger and Jace stood up and assisted them into their perspective seats before returning to their own.

"Thank you," Yolie said as Jace pulled out the seat for her. Jace smiled with a nod.

"Yes, thank you," Porsche softly remarked to Roger. There were no signs of Diva extrapolated that evening from Porsche; Only humbleness and sincere appreciation. Roger instantaneously noticed the difference and dared not question the change, only embraced it.

As the four sat there quietly sipping wine, and listening to the islands artists' perform live, it was a great way to end their last night on the island. With whispers back and forth, laughing and the enjoyment of each other's company, the only one who seemingly appeared to miss out was Drisco as he watched from afar in the bar. Leaning over, Porsche whispered something in Yolie's ear and with that, the two got up and excused themselves.

"Is everything alright," Jace whispered as Yolie got up.

"Yes, everything is fine. We'll be right back." And with a smile and kiss on Jace's cheek, Yolie and Porsche walked off, but not before Jace kissed Yolie's hand and Roger kissed Porsche's. Sitting back, Jace and Roger looked at each other and with a scotch and a long island in hand, they toasted to each other for surrounding themselves with two beautiful women and a nice evening to come.

"Good evening ladies and gentleman. We have a slight change to the program," the master of ceremonies announced. "This is a little unorthodox for this resort but we have been asked to do a special request so without further ado, here is Yolie. She will be singing a special song she wrote while on the island. Please enjoy."

And with that said, Yolie came out in a sleek, black, sparkly ballroom gown with a high slit up the right leg and a low v-neck down her front. As she started singing the song she wrote specifically for Jace, Porsche returned to the table to see Jace's eyes light up like a bright, well lit Christmas tree. Yolie's song was sultry, romantic, intense and amazing. Jace couldn't keep his eyes off of her as she sung solely to him but embraced the entire audience all the while.

No words could express how he felt that evening as he sat there mesmerized by her voice, listening and peering on every single little word. Roger took Porsche's hands in his and with a gentle kiss, she felt as though she wrote the words herself. And for that night, and that night only,

Porsche felt alive, honored and appreciated.

The evening ended with late night dancing, kissing, embracing, and an exchange of numbers. Only time would tell if and when Yolie and Jace's paths would cross again. Some would say yes and others no, but only they would know how they were going to survive the test of time; for they knew the intense feeling they shared would last forever. Yolie and Jace constructed a plan to make things happen, but dared not share it with the outside world; for only their two paths would be joined beyond the spotlight.

# About The Author

Vida Xscape is anything but ordinary. She is confident, self-assured and the epitome of a person with a "busy" schedule and an "active" lifestyle.

Working 12+ hours a day between her profession, outside projects, and volunteer/community work, she maintains a positive attitude with her vibrant, energetic personality. She chooses to surround herself with like-minded individuals. She also tries to keep things in perspective as she balances all three of her lifestyles.

As the CEO of her personal, professional and private lifestyle, she continues to aspire for greatness whether it's creating, writing, designing or giving back. Vida Xscape likes to work hard but play harder. Her mission is to help others unwind and embrace a journey filled with "laughter, fun, and romance" – Beyond the Spotlight – if only for a moment; away from their "busy" schedules and "active" lifestyles.

But regardless of how crazy her lifestyle may be, she always makes time for herself – From the BOARDROOM to the XSCAPE LOUNGE; Where Rolexes and Stilettos co-exist.